A Magical
Christmas Dream

By Mary E. Padron

Illustrated By Patrice Pendergast

Pink House Press

Collierville, TN

To Sydney,
Have a magical
holiday!
Mary E. Padron
12-15-95

A Magical Christmas Dream
Published in the United States by
Pink House Press.

Text Copyright © 1995 by Mary E. Padron
Illustrations Copyright © 1995 by Patrice Pendergast

Library of Congress Catalog Card Number: 95-92595
ISBN 0-9648284-0-5

Summary:
In this holiday story in rhyme, a little girl dreams
she shrinks to fairy-size and embarks upon
a magical adventure inside her Christmas tree.
Includes activities and discussion questions for imaginative play.

Ordering Information
This book may be ordered directly from the publisher.
Pink House Press
P. O. Box 1373
Collierville, TN 38027-1373
Phone 901-854-3888
FAX   901-854-7153

This is an original paperback printing of 5,000 books.

For Mike
because he believed in me
and for the children.

Bo
Jesse
Kelsie
Trudy
Bonny
Jordan
Bailey
Cracker
Rebecca
Christine
Julia–Ellen
Luke–Zellie
Alex–Derek
Jack–Emmett
Angel–Trevor
Johnny–Jamie
Rachel–Lucas
Carla–Danielle
A.C.–Anthony
Jacqui–Thomas
Lindsey–Amanda
Jennifer–Matthew
Laura–Jack–Jenna
Lauren–Olivia Grace
Joseph–Megan–Bryan
Joseph–Chelsea–Kayla
Annie–Jezzie–Bob–Fred
Kelly–Megan–Danielle
Emily–Cannon–Samuel
Alexandra–Jason–Brent
Kimberly–Drew–Ashley
Anneliese–Will–Anna–Ian
Alex–David–Scott–Elizabeth
Tess–Batman–Baxter–Priscilla
Erica–Alexandria–Jake–Jessica
Stephanie–Michael–Samantha
Whitney–Trey–Jeb–Jensen–Hollis
Anna Alicia–Stephanie Kristin–Andrea
Torre–Kristin–Alicia–Chip–John–Beach
Little Sister–Gypsy Rose–Sammy–Mak–Spike
Ian–Sarah–Brad–Ryan–Kaitlin–Kevin–Megan
Johnny–Whitney–Greg–Marie–Benjamen–Brandy
George–Nicole–Connie–Drew–Anthony–Terrence–Michael
Mary Lynn Acker–Susan Chamberlain–Carol Fuery–The Macray's
Guarton–Naughton–Linares–Padron–Pendergast–Curry–Duffer–Smith

Special thanks to Ron McKinney, Donna McLeod, and Don Baggett of B & M Printing
Bob Fleet at Western Paper Company–Wine, Women & Words Book Club
Thanks also to Jeanette Belew–Monica Ostrom–Missy Rosenkampff–Kim Harvell–Brenda & Jerry Smith
and Dianne Fry of Trust One Bank in Germantown

PREFACE
(The Myth of the Christmas Tree Fairies)
By Mary E. Padron

Some children believe fairies live inside Christmas trees. These fairies are good. They help Santa Claus fill stockings with candy, nuts, and oranges. Their wings, all glittery with magic dust, make Christmas trees sparkle.

However, Christmas tree fairies are mischievous. They shake the needles off tree branches and scatter them on the floor. They kick bows off packages and switch name tags on presents. When they fly about the tree, their fluttering wings make the lights blink, the tinsel sway, and the bells ring. If they become unusually active, they knock off ornaments, breaking them into many pieces.

Christmas tree fairies are thirsty. They drink the water in the tree stand and sneak sips of hot cocoa and cider. They love sweets and take tiny bites from the cookies and cakes left for Santa, especially Peppermint Cake. That's their favorite treat, for they are crazy about candy canes. They crunch and munch on them until their little hands and faces are all sticky.

Besides being thirsty and hungry, good and mischievous, Christmas tree fairies are magical. On Christmas Eve, just before Santa arrives, they fly out of the tree to look for children waiting up for Santa Claus. If they find a child awake, the fairies sprinkle magic dust into the air where it falls slowly, like a soft, golden snow. When the fairy-dust lands on little boys and girls, they fall asleep and have a magical Christmas dream.

My name is Anna Victoria,
and it's hard to believe
what happened to me
on the night of Christmas Eve.

I sat in my mother's chair,
waiting for Santa Claus.
I waited and waited, forever it seemed,
thinking of the toys Santa might bring.

But my eyes became sleepy,
though I wished to stay awake,
to serve dear old Santa
a slice of Peppermint Cake.

I heard the clock strike midnight
and knew the time was soon.
I looked outside the window
for reindeer shadows against the moon.

But my eyes became droopy;
I couldn't hold them up.
I drifted off to sleep
with cocoa in my cup.

While I was sleeping,
a dream came to me,
where I shrank to fairy-size
and climbed inside our tree.

I jumped from branch to branch.
I hid behind a bow.

I dangled from a crescent moon
and counted stars of gold.

Then I climbed a little higher
and slid down a candy cane.
I landed on a rocking horse
and held tight his golden mane.

I played tightrope on the cranberry beads
and wrestled with a bear.
I strummed upon an angel's harp
and sang a yuletide prayer.

I danced with a wooden soldier.
I touched a soft, white dove.

I crawled in and out of garland
as it swayed from branches above.

Then I climbed to the top
of our twelve-foot Christmas tree,
and there stood Santa Claus smiling back at me.
Santa's eyes were black like buttons.
His cheeks were cherry red.
His coat was made of velvet
and holly twigs crowned his head.

So I said to Santa, "Do you remember me?
I saw you at the store and sat upon your knee."

And Santa said,
"Yes, I remember.
I received your letter too.
Because you have
a cheerful heart,
I've brought toys
and candy for you."

I reached and stretched
and stretched and reached
for the toys meant for me.

But lost my balance and fell off
our twelve-foot Christmas tree.

I somersaulted.
I tumbled.
I twisted in the air.

Boom! Boom! Kerplunk!

I landed in the chair.

Now that I was wide-awake
and back to normal size,
I tiptoed 'round our living room
to look for my surprise.

Yes, Santa Claus had been here.
He came to visit me.
I found candy in my stocking
and gifts beneath the tree.

Santa must have been starving.
He loved my Peppermint Cake.
For there was not a single crumb
left on the big round plate.

Questions & Activities
For Imaginative Play

1. When Anna Victoria dreams she shrinks to fairy-size, she climbs inside the Christmas tree and plays with the ornaments. What ornaments does she play with? What other ornaments would be fun to play with?

2. Santa Claus brings toys to Anna Victoria because she has a cheerful heart. What does cheerful mean? How do you act when you are cheerful?

3. Who helped Santa eat the Peppermint Cake?
Teacher/Librarian: Has your dog ever eaten something it wasn't supposed to? Explain.
Parent: Remember when (Dog's name) ate the (item name). Prompt your child to finish the story.

4. What do you think a Christmas tree fairy would look like? In the story (see preface), what are some of the things that Christmas tree fairies do?

5. It's "OK" to dream and imagine about climbing inside a Christmas tree. But is it "OK" to climb inside a Christmas tree in real life? Why not? What could happen?

6. Ask your child/student to gently touch a Christmas tree branch and then describe how it feels. Is it soft, prickly, sticky, etc.?

7. Reread the part where Anna plays with the ornaments. As you're reading, ask your child/student to act out playing with the ornaments. Make sure this activity is done in an open space clear of objects so no one gets hurt.

8. Prepare a Peppermint Cake for Santa. Use your favorite vanilla cake mix and white frosting. Then let your children/students decorate the cake with an assortment of red and white peppermints and candy canes.

9. Read *A Magical Christmas Dream* to your children before they go to bed on Christmas Eve. In the morning, ask them what they dreamed. Ask them to tell you what their magical Christmas dream would be.

10. As part of your family, tree-decorating tradition, buy or make the ornaments mentioned in the story. Then have your children place them on the tree before reading *A Magical Christmas Dream.*

11. **Cultural/Ethnic Sensitivity Question for teachers/librarians:**
Not everyone puts up a Christmas tree because holidays are celebrated in many ways. Who would like to tell us about a special holiday custom in their family?